First published in United Kingdom 2018
by Whittrick Press
119a Seacoast Road, Myroe, Limavady, BT49 9EG

Text copyright © 2018 Sybil Allen
Illustrations copyright © 2018 Anne Montgomery
The moral rights of the author and illustrator
have been asserted

A CIP catalogue record for this title is available from
the British Library

ISBN 978-1-910225-13-4

Printed and bound in Northern Ireland
Design by Jeffers & Sons

whittrick
{ PRESS }

**Sybil and Anne wish to thank
David Lewis, Rory Jeffers and
Hugh Odling-Smee for their
enthusiasm, great input and
support in harvesting the crop.**

MIXED VEG

Sybil Allen   Anne Montgomery

Sybil Allen

Anne Montgomery.

For Michael...
"a green thought"
Sybil Allen

In memory of my
mother and father,
Maureen and Albert
Anne Montgomery

MIXED VEG

The day Tom declared war on the vegetables was a day he would never forget. It was a peaceful enough day to start with, warm, sunny – a smiling day. Tom, however, wasn't smiling. Scowling is a better word. He scowled heartily from the moment he woke up so that by lunchtime he'd had a lot of practice. When that bowl of vegetable soup was placed in front of him he was almost beside himself in a fine rage and fairly spluttered at the first spoonful. Then he stopped and, gazing into the murky liquid with little pieces of this and that floating through it, he saw no reason to go on.

"I hate soup, hate it, hate it, HATE IT – especially VEGETABLE soup. Nasty things vegetables, vile, repugnant and otherwise horrid – slimy, squashy, stringy, spongy, sweet, sour, red, yellow, green. I won't mix with vegetables." He was almost breathless and slightly dizzy. Perhaps that's why he had the sensation of the soup sucking him slowly down towards the plate and the liquid getting murkier and the bits and pieces growing larger.

Then two large hands reached out and helped him onto the rim of the bowl and over the edge gently, until he was wading through the soup and all the time it was deeper and warmer and slimier. He was wondering whether or not to swim to the other side when he realised the light had gone

and waves of soup were washing languidly over his head as if someone was stirring the bowl with a spoon.

"Who is being so thoughtless?" he wondered angrily while he was trying to keep his head above soup level.

Gradually the light returned, the other rim of the bowl appeared and the two great hands helped him yet again. He was standing on the farther shores of the soup.

The landscape here was quite different to the other side. If you expected tablecloth and table you were doomed to disappointment. Tom was standing at the entrance to a large walled garden.

It hadn't occurred to Tom to question the helping hands but now a slight cough sounded over his shoulder. He turned and there stood a man looking remarkably like a potato, with a faint greenish tinge to his complexion. His hands were indeed large, like his feet, and his nose looked like a wart.

"Top o' the mornin' to you – Sor," he said mockingly. "It's a fine mornin'. Pity you can't look more civil, especially when we've done all we can to help."

Tom was very taken aback. He wasn't used to people's remarks being so pointed.

"Excuse me, but who are you?"

"Murphy's the name – naturally!" he wheezed. "And obligin's my nature. I tried to help you over your little problem and haven't had a word of thanks, but we've wasted enough time and there's precious little of that. Come this way."

He was led up to great wrought-iron entrance gates draped with long tendrils and green shoots. Murphy coughed loudly and they waited for what seemed an eternity. A curtain of tendrils was slowly drawn back and a long, lean face peered enquiringly from behind the bars.

"Murphy here," said Murphy and winked knowingly. "With 'You Know Who'."

"Who?" said a husky voice at the same time as Tom realised he was talking to a leek.

"Tom." Murphy grinned. "On a pilgrimage. You know the sort of thing – back to seek his roots." Murphy chortled merrily to himself.

Leek never smiled. His long face seemed longer if anything. "Right," he said at last and stood back.

Murphy put his broadside to the gates and they creaked open.

"This," said Murphy, "is 'The Ideal Vegetable Garden' – everyone's always in season."

Tom gazed around in surprise. In front of him stretched an apparently endless vista of row upon row of vegetable garden – or was it in fact a large town with a main thoroughfare and side streets going off at regular intervals? It was very flat and well cared for and buzzing with life. Murphy took him by the arm and they set off together down the main thoroughfare. There were so many strange people everywhere yet somehow they also looked slightly familiar. Tom was pondering this when a tall, thin and very stringy figure in running gear came puffing heavily along the street.

"Hullo Fred," said Murphy. "Good day for exercise."

"Yup!" puffed Fred and paused to do a few press-ups. "Helps to ripen you up."

He gave a little chuckle and smiled at Tom.

"I'm training for the Marrowthon."

"Of course," thought Tom. "He's a Runner Bean."

"Like to do a few blocks young fella?"

Tom turned hesitatingly to Murphy.

"Go on," said Murphy. "I'll see you later."

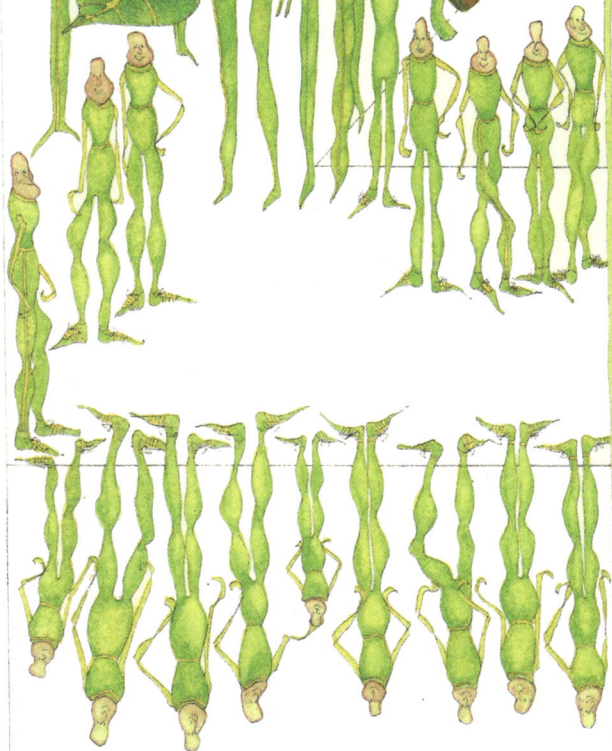

And so Tom found himself trotting in time to Fred Bean's panted breaths until he himself was panting and puffing too. They turned off the main street and followed several small turnings until Tom was sure he was going round in circles and all the time the landscape kept changing. One minute they were running between high poles laced with greenery and next, treading warily through heavy ground cover. Fred showed no sign of tiring and no interest in conversation of any kind until Tom wondered if he was meant to keep running forever. Shortly, however, they came to a halt beside a large notice saying "SHOWER" and Fred Bean turned on the tap and stood still, sighing with pleasure. Tom gasped as the garden spray started to work, showering a fine mist all around. He stood, until he was dripping wet and water was running from his hair into his eyes and down his face.

He was beginning to enjoy it. Eventually he heard Fred Bean humming a tune and then burst into song:

O fine summer spray,
O fine summer mist,
O please don't desist
When I'm in such bliss …

He began a slow, heavy dance in time to the music and Tom found himself joining in, twirling and swaying and laughing. A good spray was a wonderful thing on a lovely summer day, especially when you've been working so hard. They lay on their backs then, steaming gently in the warm sunshine and gazing at the blue sky, so perfect and so far above their heads.

"Come and meet my cousin," said Fred. "Belle. She's quite a girl! Any bean patch is a has-been patch without Belle."

Belle was indeed quite a girl – a Broad Bean in fact – and she lived round the corner from Fred. She wasn't out of bed when they knocked the door post and it took her some time to answer. She greeted them in her dressing gown and deep-pile furry slippers. A cigarette dangled from her lip. She was fat and comfortable and everything about her home was the same. The walls were plush, the bed which occupied most of the available space was plush and made you want to sink into it. Tom felt suddenly tired.

"The boy needs a little fertiliser Fred," said Belle and slowly started to prepare a long cool drink for Tom. He didn't like thinking about what it might contain but he drained the glass and it certainly seemed to revitalise him. He almost felt like another run round the block. Belle pointed to a deep cosy armchair and he sank into that instead.

"Where did you get the boy?" asked Belle.

"Murphy introduced us," answered Fred. "His name's Tom and he's on a mission, so I thought I'd take him on a quick trot around the old place."

"A mission can be heavy work," said Belle. "The run would do him good – add a little more flavour to his cheeks."

Tom had never thought of exercise as adding flavour before but he assumed it must be a good thing and anyway, what was all this chat about a mission? If he were on a mission it was the first he'd heard of it and how was he supposed to find out what it was?

"A mission," he began, but Belle put her fingers to her lips to silence him.

"Time enough," she said. "Now how about a nice game of WORMS and BEANPOLES?"

This turned out to be very like Snakes and Ladders – you slid down the worms and climbed the beanpoles and small pebbles were used as counters. It was great fun but try as he might, Tom never could climb the beanpoles as fast as Fred or avoid the worms like Belle. They were thoroughly engrossed in the game when a knock sounded on the door and Belle reluctantly got up to answer it. There stood Murphy.

"I've come for Tom," he said. "Time marches on and he has a lot to do yet. I hope you've been adding to his experience – youth's quite a short season."

"Oh – Worms and Beanpoles!" answered Belle, and Tom wasn't sure if she was telling Murphy what they'd been doing or just being rude.

"Come and see me later in your mission," said Belle and gave Tom a large sloppy kiss.

They turned right on leaving Belle's and walked some little distance until they arrived at a very grand residence. Murphy stood regarding it with some reverence. A plaque in front read "By Appointment".

"We haven't got an appointment yet so we can't go in, but this here's the royal lot – Asparagus to you. Can you see the crowns?"

Tom stood admiring the regal and lovely bed of Asparagus. It looked like a giant four-poster and the sun seemed to smile even more brightly here. Tom could indeed see a series of golden crowns glinting in the light.

Not very far away there was another bed with exotic yellow blooms and large leaves. Looking out from underneath were some very beautiful golden Courgettes. They lay luxuriously idling in the sun, except for one who was bending over and folding something into the ground around her roots.

"Good-day Ma'am," said Murphy respectfully and half-saluted. "Mademoiselle Annette isn't it?"

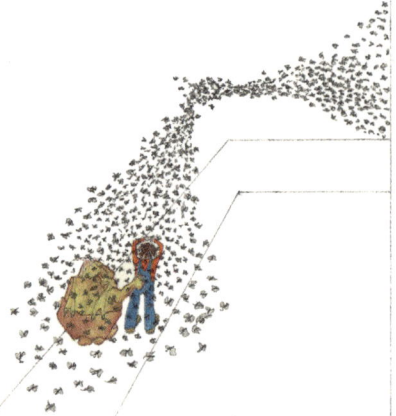

"Oo yes?" Annette looked up. "Mais oui – but to 'oom am I speaking?" Her voice was soft and she spoke with a heavy French accent. Tom was staring at her hard and he blushed when she turned her gaze on him and fluttered long thick lashes. "Can I 'elp you?"

"It's Murphy here Ma'am," said Murphy. "I'm on an Official Tour with this boy here – Tom – who's admiring you." Tom blushed again.

"What are you doing?" he spoke hastily to cover his embarrassment. "Please."

"Well, I'm just forking in a leetle, 'ow you say? – artificial manure – to 'elp bridge ze energie gap. I'm taking a special course in beautee. You can read about it for yourself in ze latest gardening magazines. Why not?" She shrugged her shoulders prettily and pouted.

Tom was still staring at her and the other bathing belles when a nudge from a sharp elbow made him turn round. A very dapper little figure smiled at him, sporting a bow tie and a saucy beret. It could only be Garlic, thought Tom as he caught a strong whiff in the air.

Garlic chuckled.

"You like ze girls then young man? And y not?" He curled his moustache round his little finger. "But zis one is for me – my fiancée. Too late old man – you must move along a leetle, experience life a leetle more." He twirled a cane and did a soft shoe shuffle, humming the while and singing:

Add a leetle more spice to your life.
Take a leetle courgette for your wife.

Mademoiselle Annette was giggling daintily and clapping her hands in time to the music. They certainly made a pretty exotic pair. Tom felt a little in the way and tugged Murphy's arm. Murphy was smiling with pleasure for the happy couple but he turned now to Tom.

"Yes, yes, time to move on, but so nice – they'll taste delicious together. Now where were we?"

They had no time at all to think for suddenly from in front came the sound of screams and groans and the rushing of many feet. An avalanche of bodies hurled themselves from round the next corner and Murphy and Tom were both knocked off their feet and trampled in the rush. Tom had no idea what was happening but the skies above his head had grown dark and a whirring sound filled the air.

"Aphids – black fly!" muttered Murphy and Tom ducked, but not before he was covered in the creatures. They seemed to be flying up his nose, into his mouth and getting tangled in his hair. He choked and Murphy, also coughing, thumped him on the back. The ordeal lasted for several minutes and then the sky grew lighter again and gradually the last of the fly crowd was vanishing down the road in the other direction – back towards Belle's in fact.

"Oh no – poor Belle!" gasped Tom. "We must warn her."

"Too late," said Murphy. "They're moving too fast. Don't worry, Belle will survive this attack just like she's done others. Sometimes we get a warning siren but the special patrols don't always manage to sound it in time. It always affects some of us more than others, but that's life." And Murphy, looking remarkably unscathed, sighed. In a few minutes, with the sun shining warmly on their backs, it was as if the black fly had never been.

Tom, however, had started thinking again of the mission he was supposed to be on. What on earth could it be and why him? Was there any point in asking Murphy? Tom looked around. There was certainly no one else to ask.

"Murphy," he began. "You know this mission I'm on – well, what exactly is it? I can't solve anything until I know what I'm solving." That sounded sensible enough, Tom decided.

"Let me introduce you to someone," was the only answer he got from Murphy as he was hustled further along the roadway.

"Looking for me?" asked a silvery old voice and Tom found himself gazing into a clump of sage.

"Our resident Sage," said Murphy. "Let me introduce Tom to you."

"Is this the young man I've been waiting for – so lo-o-ng?" the ancient voice tinkled. "Well, what can I do for you, now that you're here?"

Tom was dismayed. He knelt down.

"I thought you'd tell me what to do – and why I'm here."

"Well," said Sage and closed his eyes. His face seemed to grow out of the stem, tough and wizened and the leaves formed a thick, bushy head of hair (was it?) on top. The eyes stayed closed for so long Tom thought Sage must be fast asleep but, just as he was about to prod the old man with his finger, one eye cautiously opened.

"We-ll," said Sage again. "You're here to savour things a little."

"You mean vegetables?" said Tom.

"Those too," replied Sage. "And Life. You're here to gain a little experience, a little appreciation – and to find 'The Secret of Life'. That's all, I think – for now." He sighed wearily and closed his eyes again.

"What nonsense!" thought Tom – but then he had asked the question. Murphy, looking like he'd heard something very profound, helped Tom onto his feet. He was obviously going to be no help at all.

"Where on earth," began Tom crossly, "do you begin to look for 'The Secret of Life'?"

"All around you," replied Murphy vaguely with a slight wave of his hand. "Here, for example – why not here?"

Along the road ambled a fat Marrow, pushing a pram that was obviously becoming heavier by the minute. She was green and juicy and straining out of her clothes.

"And how's the little darlin' today? Goo goo goo." Murphy leaned over the pram and started making faces and waggling his plump fingers in the air. Long contented gurgles came from inside the pram and Tom's curiosity made him look over. The baby was remarkably like the mother, only much smaller as yet, though he did appear to be growing visibly as you watched. He lay suspended inside the pram in a hammock-type net arrangement and was pushing himself lazily from side to side. The pram covers were made out of lush leaves.

Murphy was by now making quite an exhibition of himself and the faces he made grew more extraordinary by the minute. The baby blew bubbles back at him and drops of juice ran down the sides of his fat little mouth.

"Lil sweetheart," cooed his mother now. "Oo's a good ickle pet then?"

To Tom's dismay she began to cry – large tears welling up in her eyes and running like a waterfall down her bulging body.

"If only 'is favver could have been around a lil longer to see wot a fine boy 'e produced. Ooh, I can't bear it!" she sobbed.

"There Maisie, there – don't upset yerself so. Some things aren't meant to be and we can't interfere with 'The Great Plan' now, can we?"

Murphy put a comforting arm round her shoulders and gave her a squeeze. She sobbed and bounced for a few moments more.

"Such a fine figure of a Marrow – you know 'e won every body-building contest 'e was entered for. And wot does it all come to in the end? He's probably in a fine pickle today or some jam or other – with Ginger!"

She broke down again. Tom thought of pickles and marrow jam and felt he could say nothing to make her feel any better.

"We all have to go some day now," said Murphy. "And for some it's sooner rather than later – but in the meantime Maisie, you've got to nurture the child, help him grow up like his dad. Now come, who's a big brave girl then? Let me help you over to the pram."

Murphy was really rather good at coping with strange situations, Tom thought admiringly as he watched him help Maisie from where she'd sat down heavily by the roadside. She pulled herself together, gave a little shake of her head and pushed the pram down the road.

"Poor girl," said Murphy. "It's still a very recent bereavement. Now, we'll turn this next corner, I think."

It wasn't a very long walk but Tom became aware of life in the air around him. "Enemy Aircraft" Murphy called it and Tom watched as various wasps buzzed over, interspersed with large butterflies and various other insects, hovering and rushing and dive-bombing distant targets.

"Something we learn to live with," added Murphy.

Tom thought they added a lot of colour and excitement to the scene.

Shortly they came to a large open space, a kind of square, and here they seemed to be at the centre of things. Various people sat around chatting and sipping cool drinks, laughing and waving to friends who sauntered by. Like any large city in the sun, thought Tom. His attention was riveted by two very exotic creatures leaning against a post on the opposite side of the square. At first it seemed as if they were under huge parasols but on closer inspection the parasols turned out to be very elegant hats, wide-brimmed and keeping their occupants cool even on the warmest days. The occupants were Rhubarb, looking very slim and fashionable. One was having her basket filled from a stall marked "MANURE – Fresh Today".

"They always like to keep up with the latest trends," said Murphy helpfully. "So big hats must be in fashion at the moment. You'll always see them at that stall. They love fresh foods – very snobbish you know – no canned or packaged stuff for them. Still, it's nice they care now, isn't it?"

Murphy obviously wasn't overimpressed with these elegant yet fussy ladies but Tom thought they added a delightful touch of Paris to the scene.

Suddenly the peace in the square was broken by the sound of angry voices and squabbling and everyone turned round to watch the commotion. Two young Carrots were hopping around and squaring up like boxers, all the time puffing insults as their fists shot out and punched the air near each other's faces. Tom noticed they never actually hit each other but they grew sweatier by the minute and their feathery hair flopped around in their eyes.

"Am!"

"Aren't!"

"Am!"

"Aren't!"

"Am!"

"Aren't!"

"Aren't what?" Tom whispered to Murphy.

"A better variety!" Murphy snorted. "The one on the right won 'The Seedlings Trials' as an infant and thinks he's much superior to his friend. They never stop arguing about it, little hot redheads. No control taught in schools nowadays."

Murphy was becoming quite heated himself. "Look at that gang over there now."

A small crowd had gathered round the young boxers and stood cheering them on and giggling all the while. They were a cluster of Brussels Sprouts and very matey they looked too, linking arms and clinging closely to each other.

"Now that lot can't be separated," said Murphy. "They've grown up together and where one goes they all have to go but they're just making this situation worse. That fight could go on for hours with them encouraging it. Proper little football hooligans. Teenagers!"

"Now Murphy, keep your hair on. The Heavy Mob'll soon be here and that'll send them all running." A deep warm voice was chuckling beside them.

"Oh hullo Boris," said Murphy.

Boris was a large Beetroot and looked for all the world like a Cossack with a fat belly and legs bending sideways in their effort to support him. He was smoking a cheroot and enjoying the scene in front of him immensely.

"He'll make a lovely drop of borscht some day – beetroot soup to you," Murphy said slyly to Tom and nudged his elbow. Tom was startled. It didn't seem a very kind thing to say but he didn't have long to consider it. A long blast was blown on a whistle and before he could blink there was a chorus of whistles and The Heavy Mob promised by Boris had descended on the square – a group of prize onions in fact. They launched into the fight and soon the dense smell of onion pervaded the entire square and everyone was crying and gasping for breath, fighters and spectators alike. Tom put his hands over his mouth and nose and tried to stop his tears so that he could see the Brussels Sprouts leaving the square in droves, running and falling over each other in their effort to escape the onion attack. It was as bad as the fly cloud – the War of the Aphids.

Eventually he and Murphy were forced to retreat too, the atmosphere around them was so unpleasant. Murphy led him along the opposite side of the square and down a wide street filled with various stands and gardening implements. They were quite a long way down the street before the tears stopped and their breathing began to ease.

"A very effective police force," said Tom and Murphy nodded.

"Too much power at times. We all had to suffer just then and all because of a few hooligans. Still, they've got to break it up somehow. Let's have a drink – you must be getting very thirsty."

Tom needed no second invitation, especially after the onion fumes, and so they stopped at one of the stands and were served large glasses of cool water by a tall, broad Swede. He was handsome and silent. Perhaps he knew 'The Secret of Life' and was keeping it to himself. Tom wondered about asking him but as he opened his mouth to speak the tall

Swede shrugged his shoulders and started washing up the glasses at the back of the stand.

It was then Tom became aware of giggles and new smells in the atmosphere. At the stand next to them stood a pair of pea pods, obviously twins, busily spraying themselves and each other with a selection of canisters.

"Try this scent Celia," giggled one and another puff of dust fluttered in the air around them.

"Amelia! Stop a moment. I quite liked the last. Let me savour it a little longer."

But Amelia kept trying new cans at an amazing speed and all the time her giggles became more high-pitched.

"Silly young things," muttered Murphy and coughed. "With the price of insecticide today you'd think they'd treat it with care, but oh no, and one's worse than the other, if you could ever tell which was which. In fact, they're as alike as two peas." He chuckled to himself now, pleased with his little joke. "Celia and Amelia – their poor mother never knows what they're getting up to. Now then you two, that's enough for one day – you're both stinking with that stuff."

"Oh it's Uncle Murph," giggled Celia, or Amelia. "We're only trying to find a good perfume for Mum. Any suggestions?"

"Who's that?" giggled Amelia, or Celia, pointing at Tom.

"This is Tom and it's rude to point. He's on a tour."

"Not a 'Secret of Life' one! Poor Tom. We did that at school last week. Listen, I've got a suggestion – much more interesting – have you seen the latest film showing? We've just been."

"Oh yes! Horror!" added her twin. "*Pea Selection* – it shows you peas being sorted in a canning factory. Big, medium, small – and those not making the grade at all. Horrible!"

She gave a delicious little shudder.

"Mmm, best film yet," said Celia, taking Tom's arm in a friendly gesture.

"Or we could go and watch rehearsals – that's always good for a giggle." Amelia took his other arm. "We might even join the chorus."

He found himself being jostled sideways as they tried out a few steps.

Celia, Amel-ya – Celia Amelia, that's me!
Cel-ya, Amelia – Amelia Celia, that's me!

"Come now, come," said Murphy. "Enough nonsense. If you want to see a rehearsal you've got to behave with decorum or Sir Arthur will never let us in."

The twins giggling with excitement, they all walked along until they reached a large enclosed area and Murphy banged with a stick on an upright post. After what seemed an age, a very irate, flushed and extremely artistic Artichoke appeared.

"I will NOT HAVE interruptions during rehearsals and positively NO visitors! – Oh – Murphy ... " His tone changed. "I didn't recognise you."

"So sorry Sir Arthur," Murphy was very apologetic. "We should have made a prior arrangement but we didn't really intend a visit."

"Well old chap, you've caught me at a very bad moment, you know what it's like." He raised a pair of elegant glasses on a chain and peered through them. "AND you've brought friends darling, not very convenient – but now you're here, you'd better follow me. Quietly!"

Murphy put a finger to his lips and ushered the little group inside. Sir Arthur clapped his hands and in beautiful

deep ringing tones said, "Right darlings, take a break and then we'll go from the top."

There was a great hum of activity all around them – people changing costumes, putting on make-up, fixing hair and trying out dance routines. Tom found it all quite exciting and was longing for the rehearsals proper to begin.

It began with the sensational Cauliflower Chorus. A row of perfect Cauliflower moved slowly onto the stage, their heads large and shapely, their hair curly and beautifully dressed, swirling light green cloaks around them. Tom felt he understood now why the twins were so keen on joining the chorus. A sultry Parsnip sang a long romantic song about "moons in June" and Sweet Corn was the number one comedienne. She told cheeky little jokes and laughed at them herself. She had such a sunny smile that Tom thought it wouldn't have mattered even if her jokes hadn't been funny. Some Mushrooms did a tap dance and a Tomato Chorus sang a song about Vitamins A, B and C. Then at last it was the beautiful Cauliflower Chorus again in the finale and Tom found himself standing up and cheering and clapping. It was the best show he'd ever seen. Sir Arthur smiled graciously at his enthusiastic visitor. He knew he'd a Smash Hit Success on his hands, as always. Tom would have liked his autograph, as an Artichoke signature is not something you can get everyday, but Murphy bustled the group out of the enclosure without more ado.

"Sir Arthur has notes to give the company, he's a busy man and we can't take up any more of his time. Besides you two pea pods should be hurrying on home. School got out hours ago and your mother will be anxious about you. Now off you go – pronto!"

"Thanks Uncle Murph," said the twins. "You know we just love the theatre."

"And good luck, Tom, with the 'Secret of Life' thing," said Amelia. "It's not so difficult in the end."

"As it seems in the beginning," added Celia.

They waved goodbye, linked arms and went off down the street pretending they were chorus girls.

Tom noticed the light was different now. It was later in the afternoon and the sun had shifted her position in the sky. Everything was washed in the warm mellow rays. He was beginning to feel tired too with so many new experiences following each other so quickly.

"Just the salads and the nursery to go," said Murphy, reading his thoughts. "And then the tour ends."

"Ah there you are at last," said a crisp voice. "We thought you'd never arrive."

Tom turned round and was face to face with a green young Lettuce. "We're always left to near the end," he complained to Murphy.

"It's just the way the tour goes round," said Murphy soothingly. "But next time if you like I'll start with you – though it's such a minefield treading through the salad plots."

"A minefield?" queried Tom.

"Slug pellets everywhere," said Murphy. "You don't know where to put your feet and the population changes so quickly you never know who you're talking to. Now this young man for instance – have I met you before?" Murphy peered closely at their guide.

"Lou at your service, Mr Murphy. Don't you remember me? We met last week in the seedlings bed."

"Well now you see what I mean," grumbled Murphy. "You all grow so fast and then disappear altogether."

"You wouldn't want us running to seed now, would you? We're so much better in our prime. Look what happened to my grandfather for example!"

Here Lou stopped and Tom was left to guess at the unfortunate grandfather's fate.

They had by now reached the salad beds and Lou stood back with pride to let Tom have a good look.

"That's my variety there – those lush green young things," said Lou. "Aren't we fine specimens?"

They all looked like fine specimens to Tom as he surveyed row upon row of lettuce, spring onions, radishes.

Suddenly Lou screamed and ran and Tom turned to Murphy, startled.

"Look behind you Tom," said Murphy with distaste. Tom looked and saw a large slug sailing smoothly and steadily along the surface of the soil, grinning silkily from ear to ear. Tom shuddered. Slugs were fine if you weren't a lettuce and poor Lou was such a pretty fellow.

"He's a bit like Jack the Ripper," said Tom. "Can't The Heavy Mob do something about him?"

"My dear boy, there's 'Wanted' notices on every fence post and The Heavy Mob's powerful enough dear knows, but he's not alone – capture him and there's plenty more to take his place, just like the Mafia. But don't worry Tom, Lou moved pretty fast and that chap's got to get through the minefield before he'll reach him. He could come to a very sticky end, so I don't think you and I want to hang about here. Sweet Penny Pepper will be waiting for us down at the nursery. It'll be nearly Bath Time by now so we'll need to hurry."

Sweet Penny was large and comfortable and indeed a sweet pepper – just the kind of nurse a child would want if he had to have one. She gave Tom a quick welcoming hug at the entrance to the nursery and Murphy got a tender peck on the cheek. Tom was delighted to see him blush. So Murphy had his little weaknesses too.

"Good Tom, you're just in time for Bath Time. It's always good fun to watch and I thought you weren't going to make it."

Shrieks and squeals and giggling assailed Tom's ears and he found himself in the middle of the largest Bath Time he had ever seen. Hundreds of little seedlings of various sizes and stages of growth were running around under a large spray, pushing each other about, rolling, tumbling and laughing. Sweet Penny smiled happily as she supervised, cuddling little ones who ran up to her, comforting the few who bumped themselves. A young turnip fell over Tom's foot, chuckled, picked himself up and ran off.

"Well now," said Sweet Penny, "I think that's enough for today. It's time everyone was getting into bed. Quick, quick, scramble everyone and I'll sing you some nursery rhymes."

When the little ones were tucked into bed the whole nursery looked neat, ordered and thriving. Sweet Penny's voice sang soothingly as peace descended and hung like a blanket over them all. Tom felt a lump in his throat. He was thinking about all these luscious young seedlings so full of life and happiness, growing up into sturdy prize vegetables. After that their lives were too awful to contemplate. Murphy smiled knowingly.

"Something up young Tom? Can I help at all?"

"Oh Murphy, one day they'll all be ... eaten!" Tom whispered the last word and a large tear rolled down his nose.

"And a lot better than being left to rot now, isn't it? Everything has its purpose in the Grand Scheme of Things and each of us has his fate. Now dry up those tears or we'll be having teardrop stock and maybe a little drop of boy soup." Murphy chuckled to himself. "Now if you were turned into a good drop of soup you'd like to be appreciated, wouldn't you? Remember that next time you push your plate aside."

Tom gave a little sob.

"Come on son, let's slip away before we wake up the entire nursery. It's all becoming too much for you I think."

Murphy waved goodbye across the rows to Sweet Penny who blew him and Tom a kiss in a pause between songs. They could still hear her warm voice crooning softly as they set off again, back the way they had come.

An air of dread had enveloped the salad plots. Tom could almost feel the lettuce tremble as the slug no doubt inched his way between the rows seeking a suitable victim. There was no sign of Lou. The theatre was closed when they passed and all the performers had gone home, Cauliflower Chorus and all. The Swede was tidying up the drinks stall, ready for another day and the air nearby was heavy still with insecticide where the pea twins had sampled so many cans. The garden implements had been removed too.

The square was deserted. Boris had gone, as had the Ladies Rhubarb, and all that remained was the now faint odour of onion mingled with the fresh manure from the stall. In the distance Tom could hear a mother singing to her baby – a haunting lullaby.

Perhaps it was the Cockney Marrow Mum. He hoped she wasn't quite so sad now.

Along the road a few straggling aphids fluttered past, leftovers from the earlier attack. Sage was being visited by a few bees.

"Old acquaintances," Murphy said.

They didn't stop. Even the courgettes and Garlic had disappeared – perhaps being served up together on someone's dinner plate.

"We'll soon be at Belle's," said Murphy and squeezed Tom's arm comfortingly. "But don't be surprised if she's a little under the weather. It's been a busy day for her."

Belle was rather a sorry sight when she greeted them at the door, thinner, pale and somewhat nibbled round the edges, but her smile was friendly and she looked pleased to see them.

"Murphy, something must be done about the warning system. That's the second time this month it has let us down. Just look at me. I was assaulted from all sides and not a soul to help. Still, that's enough of me – what about you Tom? Have you learned a little about life?"

She turned her sympathetic smile on Tom as she ushered him into his armchair and plumped up a plush cushion to place behind his head. They talked a while, of all he'd seen, the people he'd met and the state of the crops in the neighbouring beds. Then Belle made him another cool drink but this one made him relax and feel sleepy.

"This is for you Tom, before you go – a little present from me. Don't open it yet. Something to remember us by."

She pressed something into his hand and planted a kiss on top of his head. Then Murphy was leading him down the bean rows and towards the great gates.

"Sit down here Tom," said Murphy softly. "You're looking very tired."

He patted a large clump of Camomile ... and next to it ... grew ... Dill. Tom sat down and then lay back, his head sinking through the feathery fronds and all the time he had a strange floating sensation.

"It's been lovely doing business with you Tom. Don't forget us now, will you? And remember, everything has its purpose."

Murphy's voice faded away. The beautiful heads of Dill waved above Tom's head and the daisy-like flowers of the Camomile floated like stars before his eyes which were closing, closing, clos....

He was resting his head on the table, a bowl of soup lay to one side, a spoon was in one hand and in the other? He opened his hand slowly. He was clutching a small parcel marked 'The Secret of Life'. It was a packet of seed. Written on it were the words:

MIXED VEG

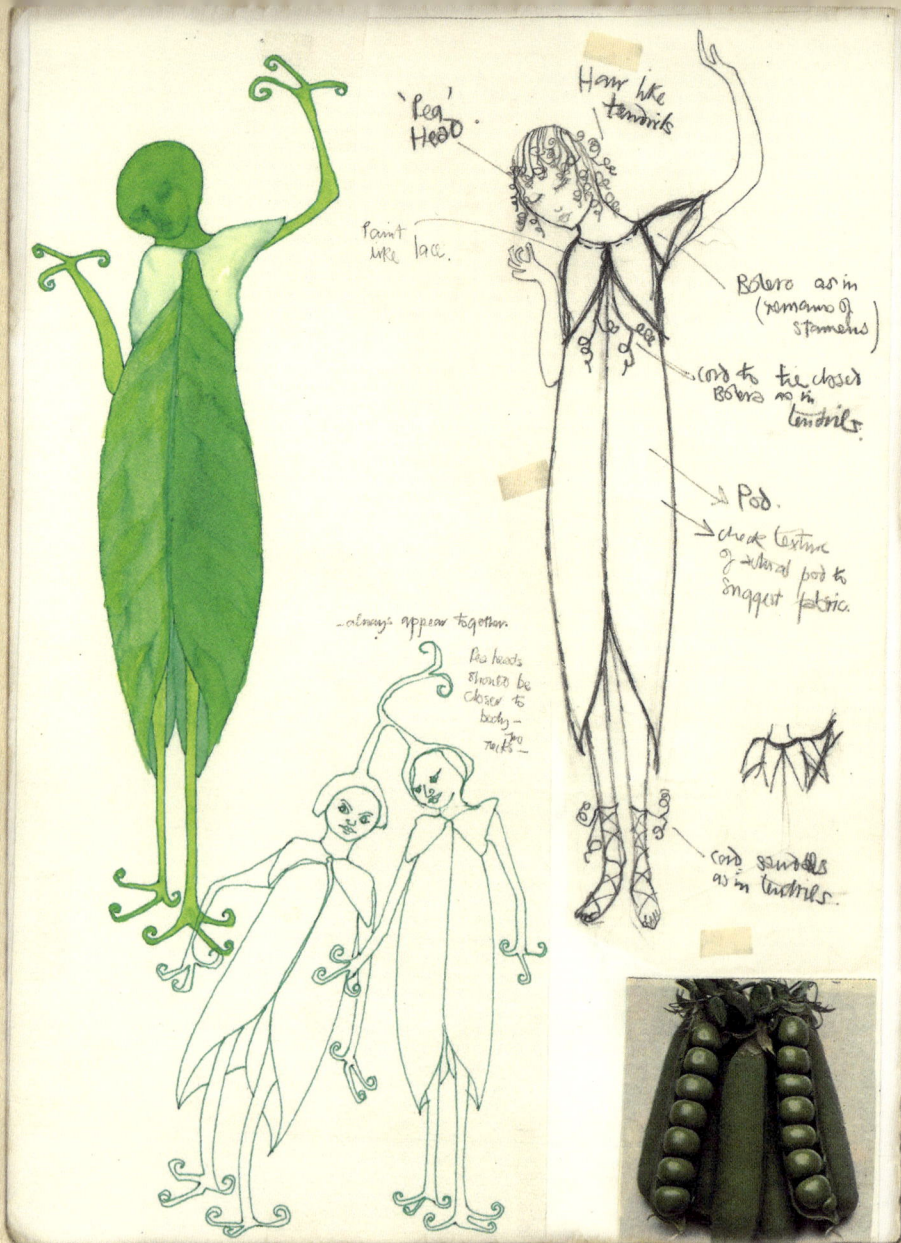

The sketch bears various handwritten annotations: "'Pea' Head", "Hair like tendrils", "Paint like lace.", "Bolero as in (remains of stamens)", "cord to tie closed Bolero as in tendrils", "Pod.", "check texture of actual pod to suggest fabric.", "cord sandals as in tendrils", "...always appear together.", "Pea heads should be closer to body – tucks?"

"I simply love drawing peas...."

A chance remark by artist and illustrator
Anne Montgomery to her actress and writer friend
Sybil Allen plants the seed for a 40-year journey.

"I'll write something for you to play with,"

responds Sybil with a smile.

A few months later, in April 1978, a typed manuscript 'MIXED VEG' arrives in the post.

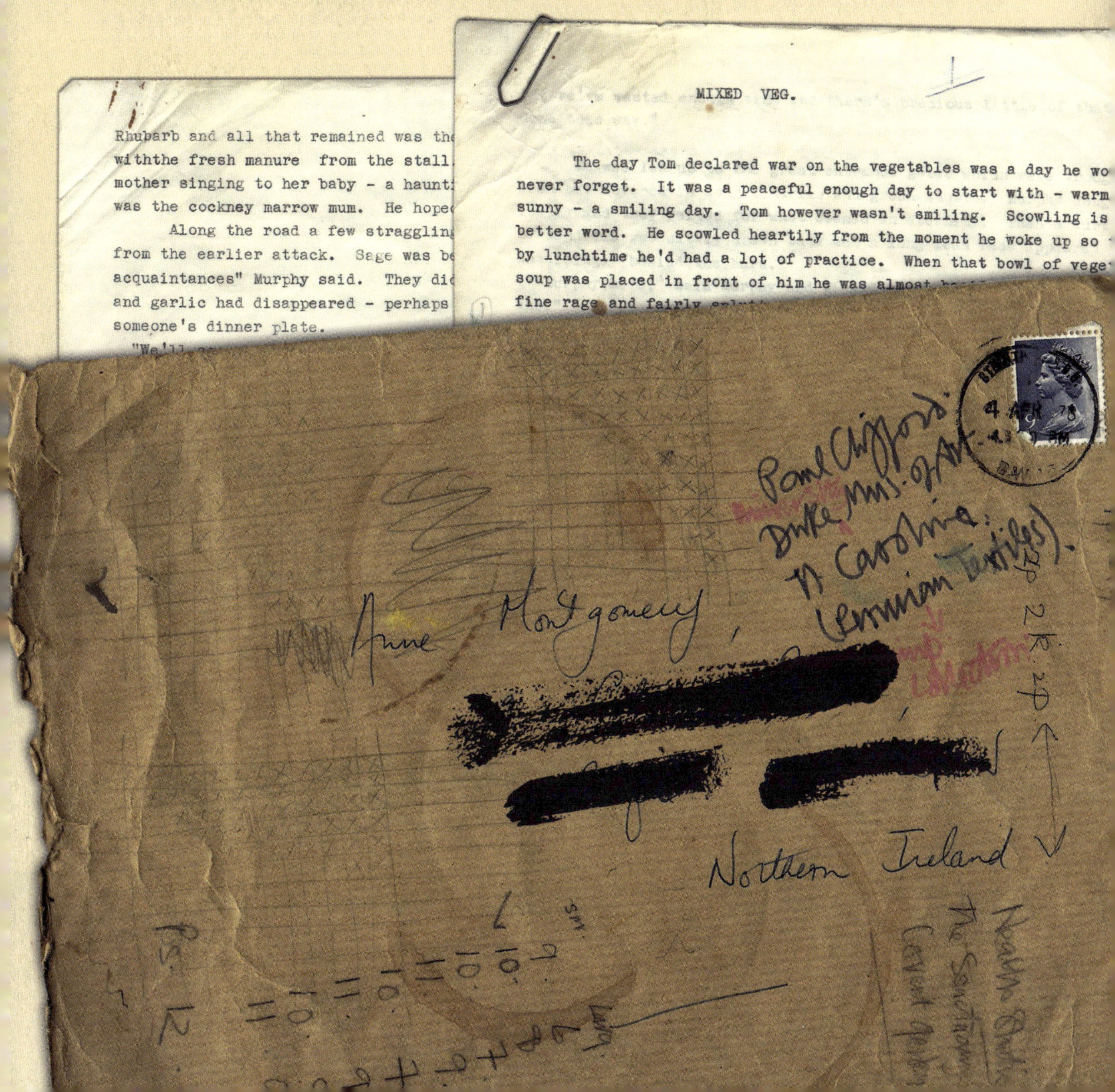

Rhubarb and all that remained was the
withthe fresh manure from the stall
mother singing to her baby - a haunti
was the cockney marrow mum. He hope

Along the road a few straggling
from the earlier attack. Sage was be
acquaintances" Murphy said. They di
and garlic had disappeared - perhaps
someone's dinner plate.

"We'll

MIXED VEG.

The day Tom declared war on the vegetables was a day he wo
never forget. It was a peaceful enough day to start with - warm
sunny - a smiling day. Tom however wasn't smiling. Scowling is
better word. He scowled heartily from the moment he woke up so
by lunchtime he'd had a lot of practice. When that bowl of vege
soup was placed in front of him he was almost
fine rage and fairly

Paul Clifford.
Duke MUS. DAM
N Carolina:
(Ermmian Textiles)

Anne Montgomery

Northern Ireland

Health Buildi
The Sanctuary
Covent Garden

Pss. 12

this photo of Sybil
is by well-known theatre
portrait photographer
John Vere Brown.

Anne loves the story of Tom and his quest for
'The Secret of Life'. It reminds her of rows of
vegetables in the walled garden of her childhood
home in Eglinton Village, Northern Ireland.

"Sybil wrote my fantasy!" she thinks with glee.

Anne gets to work...

Sybil waits... She works as an actress
and teacher in London.

Anne and Sybil
write to each
other.

Dear Sybil,
Hope you approve
of the marrow
plant pram!
love Anne...

Sybil waits...

Three years later, Anne
hands over the finished
illustrations to Sybil
at Heathrow Airport,
on her way to Papua New
Guinea to work as an
adviser on textile design.

this is Anne in 1981 showing the
readers of her local paper where
Papua New Guinea is on a map..

Sybil takes the manuscript and illustrations
around publishers in London one by one...

...One by one the publishers say thanks
but no thanks.

"The pictures are amazingly intricate and
very clever ... However, I am afraid that
I don't feel it is something we could
put out..."

"Such a project would be impossible for us
to produce economically..."

Puffin
Viking Kestrel

Penguin Books Ltd
27 Wrights Lane
London W8 5TZ

Telephone 01 938 2200
Telex 917181/2
Fax 01 937 8704

Hodder & Stoughton *Children's Books*

PO Box 705
Mill Road
Dunton Green
Sevenoaks
Kent TN13 2YI
Telephone: 0732 50111
Telex: 95122

LMJ/TD

Sybil Allen
XXXXXXXX
XXXXXXX
LONDON
XXXXXXXX X

Dear Ms Allen

    for letting us see your story, together with the accompanying
          afraid however, that such a project would be
                        and we are therefore unable
                              Bedford

"It certainly is a fun idea but I'm afraid
we don't feel it's suitable for our list."

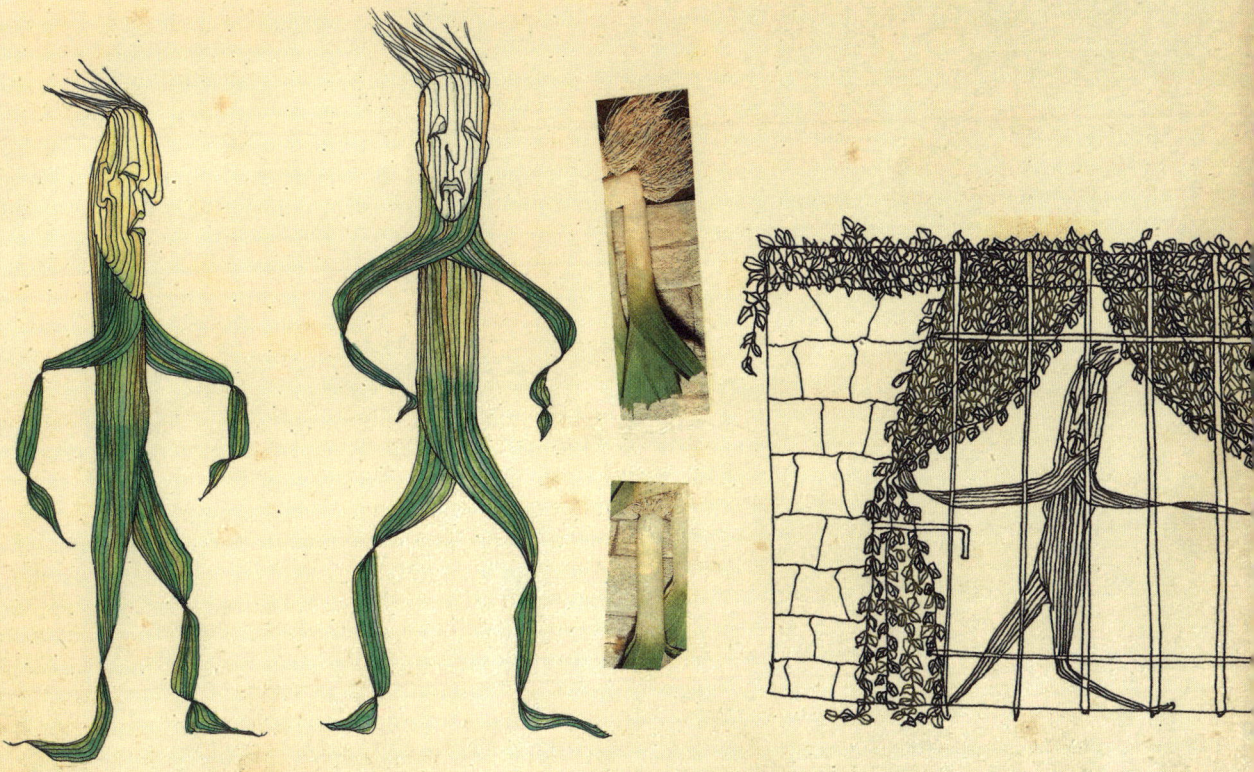

Sybil gives the illustrations back to Anne.

Life goes on. Vegetables grow and are eaten
(many times)...

Many years later, after retiring as a
senior lecturer at the Belfast School of Art,
Anne remembers the book.

And how much work went into characters like
Boris Beetroot, the boxing Carrots, Maisie Marrow,
Mademoiselle Annette the Courgette...

How she even grew a potato as a model...

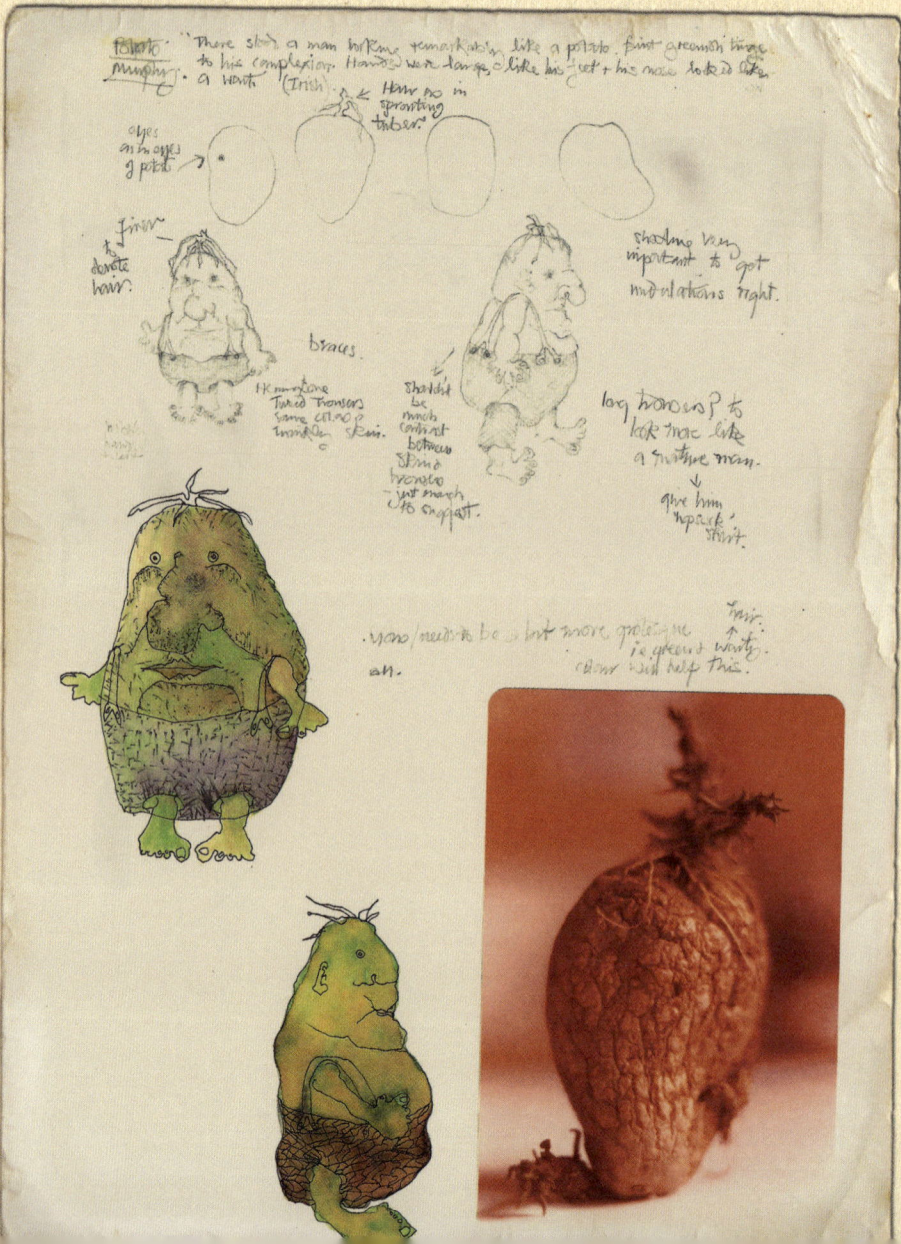

Anne dusts off the manuscript and drawings.

"Time to make a fantasy become reality!"

Anne thinks. She calls Sybil...